SOCK STORY

this
book
belongs to:

CK SMOUHA

SOCK STORY

ILLUSTRATED BY
ELEONORA MARTON

CLUNK
OH BOY PHIL... IT'S MY FAVOURITE TIME OF THE WEEK!

CLUNK
YOU MEAN OUR FAVOURITE TIME, DALE!

THUMP THUMP
WHEEEE! HEY PHIL CHECK OUT MY SKILLS..!
THAT'S AWESOME DALE-YOU'RE SMASHING IT!
THOSE AWFUL SOCKS ARE AT IT AGAIN.
THUMP

CALM IT DOWN BOYS.
DOUBLE AXEL TRIPLE FLIP!
IF YOU ROLL UP SMALL YOU CAN GO FASTER!

THUMPITY
THUMPITY
WOAH SPIN CYCLE
I'M FLYING DALE!
DUMB KIDS... THAT'S HOW YOU GET HOLES.
THUMP THUMP THUMP THUMP
THUMP THUMP THUMP

WHRRRRR
PHIL... HAHA... LOOK AT ME I'M STUCK TO THE CEILING... HAHAHAHA!
SHOW OFFS!
RRRR

PHIL...?
HEY PHIL, WHERE HAVE YOU GONE? ARE YOU AT THE BOTTOM?
BLR BLBL RBL BLRR RRRR BLLL
BLURP BLURP
HANG ON I'M GONNA DIVE DOWN TO YOU.

EXCUSE ME, HAVE YOU SEEN MY FRIEND? HE LOOKS JUST LIKE ME.
THERE'S A LOAD OF GUYS LIKE YOU OVER THERE.
HEY GUYS, HAVE YOU SEEN MY PAIR, PHIL, ANYWHERE?
OH SO YOU LOST YOUR BUDDY NOW? SURPRISE SURPRISE.
SERVES YOU RIGHT!

SCHLOOOOOOOOOOOOOOO
WHAT'S UP LITTLE DUDE?
I LOST MY FRIEND. *SNIFF*
DON'T WORRY, I'M SURE WE'LL FIND HIM. HOP INTO MY POCKET... FINAL SPIN CYCLE COMING UP!

THUMPITY THUMPITY THUMPITY THUMPITY
WAHEY! ROUND WE GO!
HEHE
SEE... IT'S NOT SO BAD... BEING ON YOUR OWN CAN BE GREAT!
THUM THUM THUM THUM
WHRRRR RRRRR

WELL... GOTTA GO... GOOD LUCK FINDING YOUR BUDDY!
CLUNK

IT'S SO DARK...
I FEEL SO ALONE...
I'VE NEVER BEEN THIS LONG WITHOUT PHIL BEFORE...
OH PHIL... I HOPE HE'S OK
WHAT IF HE GOT SUCKED INTO THE FILTER AND GOT SHREDDED??
SOB
DID I UPSET HIM?
MAYBE HE LEFT ON PURPOSE...
I JUST ASSUMED HE'D ALWAYS BE THERE FOR ME...

WHAT AM I WITHOUT PHIL?
JUST ANOTHER LOST SOCK
USELESS.
THE BEST I CAN HOPE FOR IS TO BECOME A SOCK PUPPET.
OR A GOLF COSY.
MAYBE I'LL BE STUCK IN THE CORNER OF THE WASHING MACHINE FOREVER.
GOING ROUND AND ROUND ENDLESSLY.
I NEVER THOUGHT THIS COULD HAPPEN TO ME...

CLUNK RUSTLE STUFF
SIGH IT'S NOT THE SAME WITHOUT DALE.

BLURGGLE GRGLLLL
WHAT'S THE POINT OF IT ALL...
I MIGHT AS WELL SINK TO THE BOTTOM...
SNIFF

BLOOP BLOOP
I CAN'T BELIEVE MY EYES... PHIL?? PHIL!!! I THOUGHT I'D NEVER SEE YOU AGAIN!
EXCUSE ME DO I KNOW YOU?

PHIL... IT'S ME... DALE!
DALE??? COULD THAT REALLY BE YOU? YOU LOOK... DIFFERENT!
REALLY? HOW?
YOU'RE... YOU'RE PINK!
AM I? OH GOSH! I AM!
BUT IT'S STILL ME PHIL! WE'RE STILL A PAIR... AREN'T WE...?
GEE DALE, I DON'T KNOW...

WE STILL LIKE ALL THE SAME GAMES
AND WE LAUGH AT THE SAME JOKES
AND... AND WE HAVE THE BEST SKILLS...

BUT A PAIR SHOULD BE EXACTLY THE SAME...
SAME SIZE
SAME PATTERN...
SAME COLOUR.
WATCH OUT BOYS. FINAL SPIN COMIN UP!

THUMPITY
THUMPI
TY
THUM
PITY

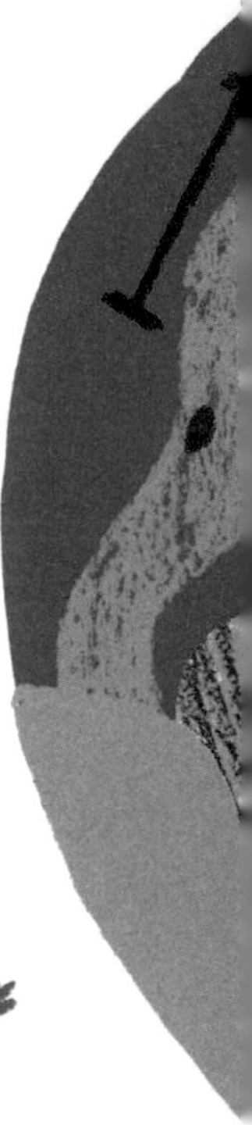

THUM
THUM
THUM
THUM
THUM

DALE CHECK IT OUT!
WHAAAA..? THAT'S AWESOME!
HEE HEE
HEHE
WHRRRRRRRRR
LET'S DO A DOUBLER!
WHEEEEE!!!
SIMMER DOWN BOYS.
OH NOT THOSE TWO AGAIN.

PANT PANT
WHO AM I KIDDING DALE- OF COURSE YOU'RE MY PAIR!
YOU KNOW, I ACTUALLY THINK THAT SHADE OF PINK SUITS YOU.

I KNOW, RIGHT?? IT'S KIND OF CHEERFUL!!

AND ANYWAY...
WHO CARES IF WE'RE
A LITTLE ODD.

SOCK STORY

Illustrated by Eleonora Marton
Written by C K Smouha

British Library Cataloguing-in-Publication Data.

A CIP record for this book is available from the British Library.
ISBN: 978-1-908714-59-6
First published: United Kingdom, 2018, USA, 2019
Cicada Books Ltd
48 Burghley Road
London, NW5 1UE
www.cicadabooks.co.uk

Illustrations made using ink, charcoal and mixed media.

Printed in Poland.

PAIR US UP!